A BRIDE FOR THE PASTOR

THE BRIDES OF PINE RIDGE

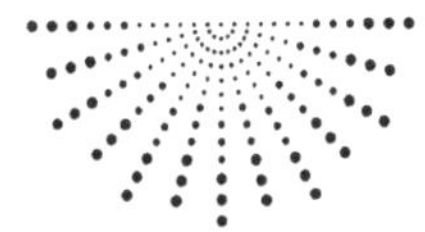

INDIANA WAKE

BELLE FIFFER

SWEETBOOKHUB.COM

WELCOME TO PINE RIDGE

Miranda Furness is coping with both the grief of losing her husband and the shock that her family are bankrupt. With four daughters, who no longer have marriage prospects, she knows she must do something drastic, if they are to survive.

An advert for mail order brides seems to be the hope she needs.

However, when they arrive in Pine Ridge, South Dakota, it seems that they have been lied to. Instead of loving husbands, that they can choose over time, they are to be auctioned to the man with the most money.

When the local pastor and a wealthy rancher intervene and rescue them Miranda is still worried about their future. What does Alex Westerman want from them?

Have they jumped out of the frying pan, into the fire?

Find out if Miranda and her four daughters can find safety, love, and happiness in this exciting new series from Indiana Wake & Belle Fiffer.

Each book is a complete and family friendly story and can be read alone, but we hope you will enjoy them all.

CHAPTER ONE

"For the last time, Debbie, you are not going out with the men to drive the cattle!" Alex swiped a hand through the air. "Why can't you accept that and leave it be?"

Debbie flinched. She didn't like making Alex angry, but he was frustrating her with his refusals. She could do this as well as the cowboys. Folding her arms, she took a breath.

"All I want to do is do something that doesn't involve housework and making meals. That's not for me."

"I've noticed," Alex grunted. "We're all aware when you're the one cooking dinner."

"Hey!"

"Well, you've proclaimed yourself to be the worst cook. That's not on me." Alex sighed. "Fine. Even though it's a year and a half too late, we'll stop you from helping out in the kitchen. And you can help out by mucking out the horses and giving them exercise."

"Excuse me? Mucking out the horses?"

"You seriously think I'm going to let you out on a cattle drive? With a herd of huge animals that could trample you to death?"

Debbie snorted. "That won't happen. I'm perfectly capable of looking after myself."

"That's not what I'm disputing, Debbie." Alex ran his hands through his hair. "Aside from the fact that your mother would kill me if I agreed to something like this. It's not going to happen, a job like the one you're asking for is too dangerous for women."

"How about you let me find that out for myself?"

"I don't need to let you find out!" Alex shouted. "I told you what happened to my mother when she went out to do it. We had no choice then, we do now. Do you think I want you to go through that as well?"

Debbie faltered. She was perfectly aware of what happened to Alex's mother; he had told her about it many times in an attempt to deter her from her desire. But that was then. This was now, and she knew she could do it better.

"It's not going to happen."

Alex groaned, slumping into his chair.

"I understand your need for independence and to show you're a capable woman. And you are, more than your other sisters. But driving cattle? That's not going to happen. I don't have anyone to watch over you, to make sure you're safe. The cowboys need to be focused on the cattle, not on you."

"I don't need a babysitter!"

"From the way you behave at times, you certainly will."

"You just said I was capable, but now I need a babysitter?" Debbie challenged him. "You're not making any sense."

Alex ran his hands over his face. He looked frustrated.

"We've been having this conversation for a long time, Debbie. And it always ends up being the same. If you want to do more on the ranch and join in with the other workers, that's fine. You show you can do it, and I'll make sure it happens. But getting on a horse and driving cattle? Absolutely not."

"But…"

"Enough! I've told you what I think, Debbie, and I'm getting fed up with you arguing about it. Don't bring this up again, because the answer is going to be the same. You are not going out there and getting in the way of animals that are far bigger than you."

"Men do it all the time!" Debbie protested. "Why can't I?"

"You mean why can't you do something that my men have been doing for years, men who were practically born in the saddle?"

"They had to learn, didn't they?"

"Enough!"

Alex slammed a hand on the desk, making Debbie jump. Now she was nervous. It was rare to see Alex really lose his temper, and she was glad it hadn't been directed at her before. Yes, he had been upset that she wouldn't let this go after more than a year, but never like this.

Alex pointed at her.

"This is the last time we're going to discuss this. It's just ridiculous that you think I will agree to it, that you can wear me down and things are going to go as you want. Whatever you did when you were growing up isn't going to work here. We don't bow down whenever someone of your caliber snaps their fingers."

"Did I say anything about my former wealth?"

"You didn't need to. It's been there under the surface. And you know it. You're not wealthy anymore, and you've been working for me for a while now. That doesn't work with me. Pestering me for months about doing something dangerous isn't going to wear me down. Andrea's been doing that for years over things even more stupid, and I haven't caved in. Now stop it and get back to work. I don't want to hear about this anymore, otherwise, I'll be letting your mother know. And you don't want her to find out what you've been begging me to do since you arrived here, do you?"

Debbie flinched. "That was a low blow, Alex."

"I've not said anything to her because I don't want her to worry, but you're pushing me, Debbie. Why you want to do something that's dangerous for you, I have no idea, but I'm not going to be a part of it. So, stop this right now."

"But…"

"You don't want me to tell your mother, do you? I know she's going to be furious that you would even try it."

Debbie scowled. Her mother really would be furious. But she was a grown woman. What was wrong with doing it?

She spun on her heel and stormed out of the study, slamming the door behind her. Oh, the man was insufferable. What was wrong with trying something new so she could be more useful? Why couldn't she drive cattle? Debbie had witnessed it from a distance a few weeks into living at the ranch, and she wanted to do it. It seemed so challenging, and freeing, it drew her like a moth to a flame. But Alex was being stubborn and refused to let her even try.

He did realize that she was an incredibly stubborn woman. Nobody said no to Debbie. They always gave in eventually. But Alex was still digging his heels in.

As if that was going to stop her from doing what she wanted.

She stormed through the house and out the front door, only to stop suddenly when she saw Andrea coming up onto the porch. Alex's daughter stopped when she saw

Debbie, arching a delicate eyebrow as she looked Debbie over.

"Oh. It's you."

"What are you doing here, Andrea?"

"This is my home, and you're asking that of me?"

Debbie snorted.

"You and Alex have been estranged for years, and you haven't lived here since you were barely grown."

"It's still the home I grew up in," Andrea sniffed. "Anyway, it's nothing to do with you why I'm here. You're merely the staff. I don't owe you an explanation."

Debbie couldn't stand Andrea. She was a snob, the complete opposite of Alex. He was humble with his wealth, and he was actually a decent person. But Andrea was pretentious and mean. According to Alex, his wife had been like that, and he didn't realize it until it was too late. Andrea just loved having money. However, she had left years ago after an argument and had vowed not to come back unless she got an apology.

There had been no apology, but she had still come back. Debbie had a feeling she knew why. She saw Andrea's look, whenever Andrea and a certain man were in the same vicinity. It made her feel uncomfortable. She didn't want to see that.

"Your father's in the study." Debbie waved a hand back towards the house. "He's not told us that you were coming."

"That's because it's none of your business."

"Only because you want more money out of him," Debbie snapped.

Andrea's lips pressed together tightly. "You don't know anything. You're just a servant girl."

"I grew up with money in our family. I know when someone like you wants something."

"But you're not wealthy now, are you? You're just a poor relation." Andrea sniggered. "I'm getting all of the money, while you're having to work for scraps."

Debbie scowled. "At least I know the value of the money I have now. It's preferable to what you're trying to do."

"I wouldn't say so." Andrea rolled her eyes. "I don't know why I'm discussing this with a servant girl. I need to speak to Father, and Pastor Hunter is coming over. I don't have time to stand here talking to you."

Debbie stiffened. "Pastor Hunter is coming? What for?"

"That's nothing to do with you," Andrea smirked. "I'm sure you would like to know what Pastor Hunter and I are up to, but you're not of the... same social status as us. It's nothing to do with you."

"I like to think of Pastor Hunter as a friend."

"I'm sure you would." Andrea swept past her. "Well, I can't stay here talking to you. I've got things to do. And don't you have floors to sweep and windows to clean? I'm sure you don't get paid for standing around talking."

Debbie watched her go, wishing she could go after the woman and slap her. Andrea was mean, and she wasn't afraid to show it. Alex wasn't mean, although it did feel like it right now. How they were related, Debbie had no idea. She had given up trying to figure it out months ago.

But knowing Darren was going to be here, and Andrea was going to be present, made Debbie feel a little nauseous. While she knew how Darren felt about Andrea - at least, she thought she did - it didn't help to see them together, watching Andrea fawn all over him. It was almost like she was doing it deliberately to goad Debbie.

This was one of the moments where Debbie wished she wasn't a servant. Because she wanted to give the woman a piece of her mind, without any repercussions. She wanted to scream at her to keep away from Alex, and to leave Darren alone. Darren didn't belong to her.

The problem was that Darren didn't belong to Debbie, either.

CHAPTER TWO

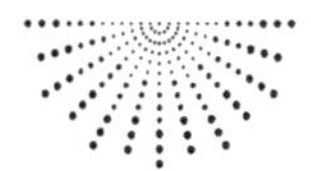

Darren saw Debbie as soon as he arrived. She was getting water from the well and was straining against the handle. She wasn't, by no means, petite, but even Debbie struggled with the well. Darren wondered why she would do it when she had almost fallen in several times.

Getting off his horse and passing the reins over to Louis, the stable boy, Darren smoothed his hair down and approached her. She hadn't noticed him just yet, her focus was still on hauling up the water.

He needed to stop being so shy and actually say something. It had been eighteen months since Debbie's family had arrived in Pine Ridge, and Darren still hadn't said anything to her. For someone who spoke to dozens of people in church when there was a service on, preaching about how they should be honest to themselves and to others, he couldn't even do that himself.

He wasn't much of a pastor if he couldn't practice what he preached. And he wasn't much of a man if he was in love with the confident raven-haired beauty and he wasn't able to say anything.

Debbie had managed to get the very full bucket to the top and now appeared to be stuck. She looked like she was trying to figure out how to let go of the handle to reach for the bucket without dropping anything, including herself. Darren hurried over.

"Let me help."

Debbie gasped and spun around, letting go of the handle. It started to spin immediately, and the bucket disappeared from sight. Then Darren heard the splash a moment later. Debbie groaned, her cheeks going red as she scowled at the well.

"Stupid thing."

"I'm sorry."

"You should be. It took me forever to get that up here." Debbie put her hands on her hips. "Why water has to be so far down below the surface, I have no idea. It's just ridiculous."

Darren frowned. He was used to Debbie being a bit spiky with her words, but she was rather standoffish.

"Are you all right?"

"Huh?" Debbie blinked. Then her face went even redder. "Oh. I'm sorry, Darren, I... I guess I'm in a bad mood."

"When is that any different?"

"That's not fair!"

Darren smiled. Even though Debbie's fire was not something he wanted to be directed at him, he did like it. She was not afraid to say how she felt. He shrugged out of his jacket and laid it over the edge of the well.

"Step back, my lady. I'll come to your rescue."

"Excuse me?"

"Just grab the bucket when it comes up." Darren gently nudged her out of the way and shook the rope. "You shouldn't be doing this on your own. Even Alex has said nobody should do this alone."

"All of my sisters are now married and off doing their own thing, Mother is busy inside, and everyone else is driving the cattle." Debbie scowled. "If Alex had allowed me to join in, then I would be out there as well."

"You're still wanting to drive cattle back here?"

"Of course."

Darren had never understood this. Debbie spoke about wanting to be one of the ranch hands, going out on the multi-day drive. Alex had, quite rightly, refused each time. Darren knew that it was not the place for a woman to be, although he was sure Debbie could give everyone a run for their money. She was a good rider and a very determined and resourceful woman.

But driving cattle was not for women. Alex was only looking out for her welfare, however, Debbie was not budging. She was tough-headed, that was for sure. Darren had to admire that.

"Is that why you're in a bad mood?" he asked as he began to wind the handle, feeling his muscles straining against the weight already. "Because you're not allowed to do what a man does?"

"What's wrong with wanting to do something men do? Women are perfectly capable."

"Yes, they are, but we all need to know our own limits. And Alex knows what is best with regards to cattle, he has a lot of experience."

Debbie snorted. "You sound like Alex. Why can't I do it? I can ride, and it can't be that difficult to herd cattle."

"I've done it when I was a younger man, and it's not easy. It's certainly not for the faint of heart."

"I'm stronger than that."

Darren didn't quite understand her. From the moment she saw the cowboys moving the cattle around, Debbie was determined to do it. She couldn't be swayed. And Darren was left confused as to why she wanted to get on a horse and herd cattle around for food. It was hard, dusty work. The long hours in the saddle left you aching and sore and bed for the night was a hollow in the ground.

"It's not a question of being strong, Debbie." Darren gritted his teeth as the handle turned more. *My, this bucket was heavy.* "Maybe you should trust Alex's judgment on this. He knows what is best for you."

"He's not my father!"

"He's your employer. And I'm sure he doesn't want your mother going after him for agreeing to what you want."

Debbie shrugged.

"Mother doesn't need a reason to go after Alex. Just looking at us the wrong way sets her off. I've never really understood why."

Darren did. He had been seeing it for the last year. Miranda was in love with Alex, and she didn't like it. Whether it was because she didn't want to fall for her employer, the man who had rescued her, or because she felt like it was a betrayal of her husband's memory, Darren wasn't sure. But Miranda certainly felt guilty about it. If he were in the same position, Darren would probably feel the same.

How would her daughters feel, how would Debbie feel if this came out? "What would you say if anything happened between your mother and Alex?"

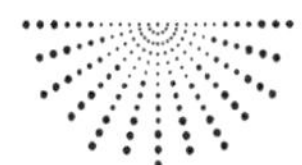

CHAPTER THREE

"What?" Debbie looked across at Darren.

"You know... if Alex and your mom... courted."

Debbie's mouth dropped open. "Those two... what... no way!"

"Well, you haven't seen what they're like all the time."

"Of course, I do. They fight."

"Not all the time." Darren got the bucket to the top and managed to tie off the handle to keep it in place. "I've seen them actually be civil to each other."

"That doesn't mean they're in love with each other." Debbie arched an eyebrow at him. "Are you trying to get another couple up the aisle, or something, Darren? Do you have weddings on your mind all the time or something?"

"Well, you can't beat a good wedding." Darren leaned in and grabbed onto the bucket, heaving it onto the wall. "It's usually a good day, and everyone walks away happy."

"Not everyone."

"For the most part." Darren paused, glancing over at her. "Do you think you'll ever get married, Debbie?"

"What?" Debbie's eyes widened, her mouth dropping open. "Why would you ask that?"

"I... I'm just curious, that's all."

Why was he even asking this? Darren shouldn't have even thought about it, and he certainly didn't want to think about someone else getting married to Debbie. That would really be a difficult ceremony to get through. Darren felt nauseous at the thought of seeing someone who wasn't him finding love with Debbie.

If you don't like the thought of it, why don't you actually tell her the truth, you fool?

Debbie was still staring at him when Darren heard a familiar voice coming from the house. His heart sank as he looked past Debbie and saw Andrea standing on the porch. She was watching him with a seductive smirk, beckoning him over.

Now Darren guessed there was another reason why Debbie was upset. The two women did not get along. Andrea liked to make people feel uncomfortable and treated everything like it was a competition. And she seemed to be more focused on Debbie. Darren wished that Andrea would just back off, but Andrea had a hard time taking hints.

Especially when it came to him. For some reason, Andrea desired him. Darren had no idea why, as he hadn't cared much for Andrea before, and he certainly didn't now. But she just wouldn't listen.

She had been estranged from Alex for a long time, and those years had been very peaceful. Now she was back, and Darren wanted her to leave again.

"I think Miss Westerman wants to talk to you," Debbie said curtly. "You'd better not keep her waiting."

"I think I would prefer to go back to town."

"After Alex invited you to dinner? That would be rude."

Darren frowned. "Andrea wasn't invited to dinner, was she?"

"No, and she won't get anything even if she wants to stay. Mother refuses to make anything for her."

"How does Alex react to that?"

"He said if they weren't expected for dinner, they would get nothing. It doesn't change because of his daughter."

Darren was surprised at that. While his friend and Andrea weren't that great in terms of their relationship, he thought that Alex wanted to rebuild something. It didn't sound like it if this was what Debbie was saying. Then again, Miranda didn't care for Andrea, either, and she wouldn't be backing down from that.

"You'd better go in," Debbie said, stepping towards him and taking the bucket. "I'm sure she doesn't want to be kept waiting."

"Debbie..."

"I'll be fine on my own." Debbie lifted the bucket off the wall, her hands brushing against his. "I can take care of things now."

"Are you sure?"

Debbie paused, glancing back at him with a flicker in her eyes. Then she gave him a small twitch of a smile, and she half-walked, half-staggered towards the side of the house. Darren watched her go, wanting to go after her.

A pointed cough had him jump and look around. Andrea was approaching him, wearing a wide smile.

"Aren't you going to come in, Darren? Father said he was waiting for you." She reached for his arm. "How about you escort me in?"

"I think you can escort yourself just fine," Darren pulled his arm away. "You don't need to be touching me to do it."

Andrea pouted. "You're not much of a gentleman, Darren. I thought pastors were meant to be gentlemen."

"Not this pastor. Now, if you'll excuse me, Andrea?"

Darren stepped around the young woman and headed towards the house, wishing that he could go after Debbie and spend more time with her. Then again, his shyness that came up whenever he was around her would more than likely get in the way again. Then both of them would be embarrassed.

Darren more than Debbie. It had been like that for the last year and a half. And Darren couldn't bring himself to find the courage to confess his feelings... or even give her a hint.

"Now this is one way to pass the evening," Alex declared as he settled back in his chair, crossing his legs at the ankles. "Dinner, drinks, and watching the sun go down. I can't think of anything better."

Darren chuckled. He could certainly agree with that. When Alex's grandparents had got the property in the land grab, they had built the house specifically so the back porch was facing the west. They had wanted to see the sun setting every day, his grandpa saying it was one of the best things in the world to see. After making friends with the older man and spending a lot of time at his place, Darren could see why.

He was feeling a little better now that Andrea had left the house. Alex was looking the same; he had been rather agitated to have his daughter in his home, but he hadn't said anything about why Andrea was there. Darren wasn't about to pry, not just yet. Alex would tell him eventually about it. With Andrea, they needed a while to calm down before discussing anything regarding her. She was exhausting.

There was a movement to Darren's right, and he looked around to see Debbie coming out, carrying a basket and heading towards the vegetable patch. He couldn't stop himself from watching her, admiring her long, graceful strides across the backyard. She didn't look their way, keeping her head high. There was something stiff and frustrated in her body language, and Darren wished he knew what he could say to make her feel better. Seeing her smile did make him better.

"Eyes back in your head, Pastor."

"Hmm?"

Alex chuckled.

"As much as I agreed that Miranda's daughters could stay here and work until they found husbands, I didn't expect them to disappear so fast. And I've grown accustomed to having them around."

"I'm sure Miranda will be delighted to hear that."

"She'll probably accuse me of taking advantage of them as cheap labor," Alex grunted. "She likes to find something to get upset at me about."

Darren sipped at his drink. "You pay them well, that is not the issue... when are you going to tell Miranda?"

"About what?"

"I thought you were good at talking cryptically, Alex. You should know what I'm talking about."

It didn't take a smart man to know that Alex was in love with Miranda. Despite the supposed animosity between them, it was clear that they each had a mutual respect for the other person, and they did work well together. Darren was surprised that his friend, who was normally so confident and not afraid to say what he had on his mind, would be so nervous about displaying how he felt.

Then again, he did enjoy the little dance between the rancher and housekeeper. It was fun to watch.

"Don't even go there, Darren," Alex groaned. "Leave it be."

"What? You keep teasing me about Debbie."

"Well, it is amusing. You are in love with her, and you haven't said a word to her about it. Everyone else has admitted their feelings, even stubborn Ed. What's holding you back?"

Darren frowned. "There's nothing holding me back."

"That's rubbish, and you know it." Alex gestured towards Debbie, who was now kneeling in the vegetable garden, picking at the plants. "She's beautiful, although she's stubborn and will probably keep you on your toes. Life in your house with her as the pastor's wife would certainly be fun. But she's a good person, even if she drives me insane."

Darren could see Alex was trying to drive it forward. Even with his frustrations about Debbie wanting to go out with the other men herding cattle, he was still fond of her. Alex had come to see all of the Furness daughters like his own daughters. Darren could certainly agree that Debbie and her sisters behaved more like daughters than Andrea ever could. They didn't care about money; they were just happy to be given a situation where they weren't forced into marriages they didn't want.

He could still remember that day when he and Alex found out what Jago was up to. The conman had been going on about how he was going to make things big, and how he had ways to get more money coming in. At the time, Darren had just rolled his eyes and ignored him; Adam Jago was always coming up with different things to make money. Never did he think he was going to bring in women and sell them off at auction like they were hunks of meat.

If Alex hadn't sprung into action, Miranda and her daughters would be married off by now to undesirables who would treat them like trophies and maids, and pretty much degrade them. Coming from the life they had been brought up in, that would have been an all-time low for them.

They were now much better off. Now Debbie's sisters were married, and they were happy.

Leaving just Debbie. And Darren knew it wouldn't be long before someone turned her head. So why wasn't he saying anything to her?

Because you're a coward, that's why. Confidence in front of several dozen members of your congregation isn't the same as confidence in front of one woman.

There was a movement in the doorway, and Darren looked around to see Miranda Furness stepping out onto the back porch. He shot to his feet, his heart racing. How long had she been standing there? Did she hear them talking, did she know? If she did, what would she do?

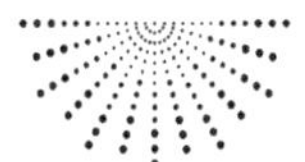

CHAPTER FIVE

Miranda wasn't looking at him but was focusing her cool stare on Alex. "I've finished clearing up. Is there anything you need before I go on with my work?"

"It's fine, Miranda. I'll get anything I need." Alex gave her a small smile. "Thanks for dinner. I do appreciate it."

Miranda didn't immediately respond, but Darren saw how she started blushing. Clearing her throat, she turned and caught Darren's eye. Nothing was said between them, but Miranda arched an eyebrow and glanced at her daughter. She gave Darren a pointed look before she went back indoors.

Alex chuckled. "Looks like Miranda's made her opinion clear on you and her only unmarried daughter."

"I didn't see any opinion made."

"I did. She was telling you not to be so stupid and actually do something about talking to Debbie."

Darren snorted. "You and Miranda seem to have figured out a silent language between you."

"Well, she and I are in agreement about you two. Even though we've never discussed it. Besides," Alex raised his glass to his lips, "she's a better match for you than my daughter. I have no idea why Andrea is infatuated with you, but you're not good together."

Darren felt bemused as he settled back in his chair.

"I'm surprised you're trying to get the object of your daughter's desires to be with someone else. Normally, parents want the best for their children."

"I know my child. You two aren't a good match. She would not be a good pastor's wife."

"And Debbie would be?"

"She's shown she can adapt to any situation she comes across. Andrea has one world, and it doesn't shift. Plus, I know she doesn't like you. Why would I try and match up two people who are going to be unhappy down the line?"

Darren hadn't thought about it like that. He had been raised that parents should always be on the side of their children. His parents had instilled that into him. So, to hear Alex say he wasn't going to support his daughter was surprising. Then again, considering how spoiled Alex's wife had been towards Andrea, and how she was as a grown woman, it was no surprise. Alex didn't like spoiled people; he was one of those people who worked hard for his money and saw value in money. To see someone who thought that it was for flashing around, buying nice things, demeaning others, and to show off their status... felt wrong.

Darren didn't see the point in it, either. Andrea was a little too obnoxious for him. Why she had her sights set on him, he didn't know, he found it confusing. Darren had never done anything to make Andrea think they would be a good match together.

"Do you know why she's so focused on me?" he asked. "I've been trying to figure it out for a while, but I can't think of anything logical."

"It's Andrea, so it doesn't have to make sense. I gave up trying to figure out what she's up to a long while ago."

"Including why she wants to be around you?"

Alex grunted. "She probably wants more money. When she left, she said there was nothing to bring her back as I wouldn't give her money whenever she clicked her fingers. Now she's back, and keeps asking for money."

Darren frowned. "She left because you wouldn't bow down to her, and now she's back expecting you to bow down? How does that work?"

"I'm not sure. Maybe it's because she found out that I had five extra people in the house, and she thinks I'm using my money on them. Perhaps she's threatened that I'm spending her inheritance on others but not her, and she wants it."

"You think that's it?"

"It's the only thing I can think of." Alex smiled. "Maybe that's why she's focused on you. You were a part of rescuing the ladies. Maybe she thinks you're rich as well."

"Me, rich?" Darren barked out a laugh. "I'd love to be, but that's not my focus right now."

"No, your focus should be on a certain Furness girl."

"Alex…"

"What? It's been eighteen months now. Maybe you should actually do something about it."

Darren cleared his throat and shifted in his chair.

"It's not that simple, Alex. You know that, seeing as you and Miranda…"

"You let me deal with that. Focus on yourself, Darren."

"As your pastor…"

Alex held up a hand.

"I'm not going to have you preach at me about that, Pastor Hunter. You let me deal with my personal life."

"As long as you leave my personal life alone as well," Darren shot back.

"All right, fine." Alex shrugged. "But you should say something soon. Even with her stubborn streak, Debbie is a beautiful woman. It won't be long before someone comes along and turns her head. Then you will have missed your chance."

Darren scowled. "You think I don't know that?"

"You clearly don't, seeing as you've done nothing."

Darren sighed. "I wish people would stop commenting on my lack of a love life."

"It's only because we care. Also," Alex winked. "It is quite amusing to see you so flustered over a woman. I didn't think I'd see you like this about someone."

"I'm not a spectacle, Alex."

"I never said you were. But, let's just say, I find it quite amusing that you have two women who want you when you're normally so shy. It shows that there are quite a few people who find the sweet, gentle type attractive."

Darren groaned. "You're really enjoying this, aren't you?"

"Of course, I am." Alex gestured across the yard. "Just don't take forever with Debbie. Otherwise, you'll regret missing your chance."

Darren had a feeling he would. He just wished that he had the confidence to go out there and act. What would he do if he lost her?

CHAPTER SIX

ebbie slumped against the tree trunk, staring in despair at the cattle that were by the river. They were taking their time and seemed in no hurry to go anywhere.

They certainly hadn't been impressed when Debbie had tried to get them to move along.

This was supposed to be easy. Debbie had gone out riding and had found a small group of cattle that had somehow come away from the rest of the herd. Nobody seemed to notice that they were missing, and she had seen it as a perfect opportunity. This would be just what she needed to show that she could do what the men did.

All she needed to do was to drive them in the direction of the ranch, there were just six large cows, and she would be proving to everyone that she could do it. She deserved to be out there with the others, just as she had always wanted.

But now it was becoming clear that this was not something she could do. Not on her own, certainly. It was very scary going up to six animals that looked like nothing was going to get them to budge. They seemed like placid beasts, but coming up close without a fence in the way was more alarming than Debbie thought it would be. She had attempted to get the cattle to move, using the shouts and noises she had heard back at the ranch, but they just stared at her. Getting closer on her horse hadn't worked well, either, as her horse had been very nervous getting within reach of those horns. And the noises as she neared the cows had been terrifying.

Now Debbie was beginning to regret saying she could do this. As soon as she witnessed it happening, it fascinated her. She liked the idea of being in charge and showing some courage; those animals did look unnerving. It would show that she was stronger than people thought she was.

Now, she had been given this chance, and it wasn't happening. It was all going wrong. Instead of doing the sensible thing and getting someone else, Debbie had decided to try and move them on her own.

She felt like an embarrassment. At least nobody had seen how she had been knocked out of the saddle when one of the cows scared her horse to the point she had to grab onto the pommel. It didn't help, the horse twisted quickly and skillfully and she was sent tumbling to the ground. Her leg was hurting from getting caught between the horse and the cow or the fall. Her knee was throbbing, and Debbie didn't want to look to find out what the damage was.

Her horse was further down the river, grazing like it hadn't just been jostled. Debbie didn't think she could chase after it.

This was a mess.

Alex was right. She wasn't cut out for doing this. Debbie had been so sure that she could do this or anything, and she had refused to listen. Alex was the one who had been doing this for years, so why had she thought she knew better?

She would do whatever Alex wanted in the future, as long as she didn't have to do something so stupid as this ever again.

Debbie knew she needed to get back. She had to, otherwise, her mother was going to wonder where she was. It was Karen's birthday, and everyone was coming to the ranch for dinner. Debbie had to be there, or Miranda was going to be upset.

She's going to be more upset when she finds out what you tried to do.

Getting back to the ranch was going to be interesting if she couldn't move very well. And if her horse was still skittish...

"Debbie!"

Debbie looked up, her heart in her mouth when she saw a familiar figure coming along the riverbank. Oh, no, not this. Of all the people to come upon her, why did it have to be him?

Darren slowed his horse as he reached her, looking at the cows before he turned back to Debbie with a bemused expression on his face.

"Dare I ask what you're doing?"

Debbie could feel her cheeks getting warm. She swallowed. "It's not what it looks like."

Darren didn't respond for a moment. Then he dismounted, patting the horse on the neck before approaching her. He didn't look upset about anything. That was the thing about Darren Hunter; he never placed judgment. The man knew how to listen. Debbie liked how he could listen to her rant for so long and not be upset about it.

It was rare to find someone who could listen the way Darren did, back where she grew up no man listened, they were all too eager to talk about themselves. Debbie had thought it was not something a man would do.

She took a deep breath. "I was trying to bring the cattle back to the herd."

"You were?"

"I found them here," Debbie went on quickly as Darren raised an eyebrow. "I didn't lure them away. I thought if I could get them back on my own..."

"Then you could show Alex what you can do."

Debbie nodded.

Darren sighed. "Debbie, there is a reason cattle ranches have people go out in groups. Nobody does this on their own, mostly because it's dangerous." Darren crouched before her, his eyes narrowed as he stared at her. "Another reason why Alex won't have you do this is that he knew you would go off on your own. Even if you were the toughest woman alive, you wouldn't be able to do this alone without some harm coming to you. Did you think about that?"

Debbie felt like she was being scolded. She looked away. "I guess I didn't," she mumbled.

"Then why would you do it? Why would you try and do something dangerous? I didn't think you were the type to take those risks, but clearly, I was wrong."

"I just wanted to show that I..."

Debbie's voice faded. She didn't know if she could actually do it and tell Darren the truth. Darren tilted his head.

"Show what? What were you trying to prove?"

Debbie had told Darren a lot of things, mostly because he could listen. And he did give good advice when asked. He was the person she turned to for guidance, mostly because she wanted to be in his company. But now her words were failing her. She swallowed.

"I... I don't think I can say."

Darren looked like he was going to push it, but he didn't. Instead, he sighed and looked her over.

"Are you injured?"

"I got my leg caught between the horse and one of the cows and I fell."

"Does it hurt?"

"A little bit." Debbie held out a hand. "Can you help me up? I want to get up."

Darren frowned, but he took her hand and helped her to her feet. Debbie gingerly tested her leg, grimacing as something in her knee protested. She tried again, and it started hurting again, but not as much.

"All right?" Darren asked.

"Not really." Debbie flinched and tried to fight back the tears. She felt so embarrassed. "It hurts."

"How bad is it?"

"I think I can walk on it, but I'm going to be sore." Debbie straightened up. "I think I'll be all right."

Darren didn't look convinced. "I don't know…"

"As long as I get back into the saddle, I'll be fine." Debbie sighed. "I suppose we're going to have to go back to the ranch and tell Alex about the loose cattle. I'm not going to get them back on my own."

"It's probably for the best." Darren looked over at the cows. "Although we'll have to be quick. I don't see them waiting around for us."

"I suppose."

It was then that Debbie realized that she was still holding onto Darren's hand, but neither of them seemed to be interested in moving away. And Debbie had to admit that she liked Darren holding onto her hand like this. His touch was warm and soft, and the tingles that were going up her arm were very pleasant.

"Oh. Right." Darren flushed a light pink and let go of her suddenly, jumping back and looking uncomfortable. "Sorry, I…"

"No, no, it's…"

"I didn't mean…"

"Darren, it's fine." Debbie managed a smile. "I'm not going to get cross if you hold onto my hand for too long."

Darren still looked unsure. He swallowed and rubbed the back of his neck. "I... I think we'd better get back to the ranch. Alex will know what to do about this."

"I suppose." Debbie glanced towards her horse. "Can you help me get into the saddle? It's my dominant leg that hurts, so I might need a lift."

"What? Oh, right." Darren cleared his throat. "I'll help. I... I'll see what I can do."

Debbie had never seen a man go from one emotion to another so fast, but she wasn't about to complain. It was actually endearing, even if she was making him uncomfortable. It made her want to kiss him.

Wait, where did that come from? She needed to rein that in.

Licking her lips, Debbie hobbled towards her horse. So much for being strong and confident. Being around Darren threw that right out of the window.

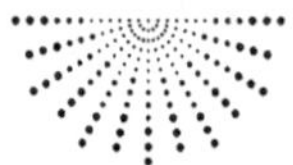

"How's Debbie doing?" Darren asked as Miranda came down the stairs.

The housekeeper sighed.

"She's just got a bruised knee. It's going to be a while before she can walk properly, but there's no real harm done."

"She thought it was broken."

Miranda shook her head. "Debbie was always the one who thought something was broken. And the one who ended up in scrapes as a child."

Somehow, that didn't seem surprising. Darren was glad that it wasn't anything more than bruises; from the way

Debbie had been when she walked, moving very gingerly, it could have been anything. At least it wasn't serious, but Darren had been worried.

He looked up the stairs. As soon as Miranda had seen her daughter limping through the door, she had immediately shuffled her up to her room. Darren had been left in the hall, waiting for Alex to come back after rescuing the cattle that decided to go for a wander from the rest of the herd. His friend wasn't going to be happy about that, nor was he going to be happy that Debbie tried to do something about it herself.

Then again, it may have been good for Debbie to hear Alex say 'I told you so'. It was not nice, but she needed to have it done. At least Debbie was admitting that it had been too much for her. A smile crossed his face, the gentle woman was tough, and if anyone could do it she could, what she didn't realize was that the men had been working toward it for months and that they were shadowed when they first went out on a drive. Given the same experience, she could do this but he didn't want her to. Men got hurt on cattle drives and she could too.

"Why is Debbie so sure that she can be a rancher like everyone else? It seems a bit strange that she's so determined about it."

Miranda pinched the bridge of her nose.

"It's best that Debbie talks to you about it. It's not really for me to say why she's like this."

"She's your daughter. Surely, you know."

"And I think it's for Debbie to say, not me." Miranda paused. "You can go up and see her, but only if you keep the door open."

Darren blinked.

"You think I would be inappropriate with her? Have you forgotten who I am?"

"I have to protect my daughters, and you are going to be in her bedroom, Pastor." Miranda gave him a sharp look. "I'm not about to have things made more complicated for us."

Darren understood that. Although it did smart that she didn't trust him. He ascended the stairs, going to the door that was slightly ajar. Through the gap, Darren saw Debbie sitting on her bed, her knee propped up on a pillow. She looked a little pale, but no worse for wear after their bumpy ride back to the house.

He knocked gently on the door. Debbie looked up as he entered, straightening up with a widening of her eyes.

"Does Mother know you're up here?" she hissed. "You could get into trouble!"

"Your mother allowed me to see you." Darren hesitated, and then approached the bed, sitting on the edge of the mattress. "How are you feeling now?"

"My knee is still really sore, but Mother says I'll live." Debbie adjusted her skirts. "It's nothing out of the ordinary for me. I can be quite clumsy."

"Your mother hinted about that."

"I'm sure she did. She and Father were always shaking their heads whenever I hurt myself. I did it so often that it ended up being no surprise."

Darren could imagine. From the moment he first met Debbie, he guessed that she could end up hurting herself without really trying. She couldn't go on a walk without her ankle rolling on her. It was almost like a regular thing for her.

He was just glad that she was back at the ranch and safe.

"Can I ask you something, Debbie?"

"What?"

"Why are you so determined to be a cowboy, a cattle herder?" Debbie frowned.

"Why do you want to know now?"

"I've always wondered, but before you were sure that it would happen. Now you've admitted that it's not feasible, I wanted to see if you would give me an honest answer."

For a moment, he thought Debbie wasn't going to answer him. She bit her lip, and Darren tried not to get distracted by her mouth. He really needed to focus when he was around her. This drifting never helped.

Finally, Debbie sighed. It looked like she had decided that she had to admit the truth, but she was worried about what it made him think of her.

Should he have pushed this? Did he really want to know?

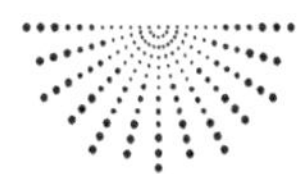

CHAPTER EIGHT

Darren found he was holding his breath. Desperate to learn more about her motivations but afraid to hear them.

"When I was growing up, I was... well, there were people who weren't very nice. They chose to call me names, mostly. Called me weak and pathetic. It's been happening since I was about ten."

Darren blinked. "You were called stupid names as a child, and that made you want to drive cattle?"

"I know it's ridiculous, but it looked like something I wanted to do. Something exciting." Debbie winced. "That was something else I had been called as well.

Boring. I was considered the least interesting daughter out of my sisters."

"And because of that, you wanted to prove a point."

"Something like that. I wanted people to see me as the interesting, exciting sister. That I was strong and capable. And I, foolishly, thought this was going to work."

"By doing something that predominantly men can do?"

"I guess I didn't think it through." Debbie looked away, her hair falling across her face. "I just wanted to show people that I was independent, able to do anything, and nobody seemed to care. I thought Alex didn't care and saw me as weak."

"That's the thing. He doesn't see you as weak."

"I know that now." Debbie sighed. "I suppose he's going to be really upset with me about this. I did try and do something he had been telling me not to do for some time."

"He's upset that you even attempted it, but I think he's more relieved that it wasn't as bad as it could have been." Darren paused. "He's probably going to give you a scolding, though."

"I guess that's the best outcome."

Debbie looked downcast. Darren could understand the need to be a person she was desperate to be, but it almost ended up with her seriously hurt. He was glad that he had chosen to go looking for Debbie and pretend it was a chance meeting. How he was going to explain why he was riding out on Alex's land, Darren wasn't sure, but he could think on his feet.

It was probably best that it worked out this way; Debbie was probably going to think he was odd. If she didn't already.

"Are you mad at me?" Debbie asked.

"Why would I be mad at you?"

"Because of what I did."

Darren smiled. He reached out and touched her hand. "I don't think I could be mad. Frustrated, yes, but not mad."

"Really?"

"Are you concerned that I will see you differently?"

Debbie bit her lip. "You probably think I'm a silly girl."

"I think you're strong, but you're trying to be a little too strong. It's best that you take a step back and take a deep breath before you start afresh."

Debbie didn't respond for a moment. She still looked embarrassed, though. Darren squeezed her hand.

"You're just trying too hard. There's nothing wrong with being yourself instead of trying to prove something to everyone else. Doesn't that get to be difficult after a while?"

"I... I suppose." Debbie was staring at their hands still joined. "I wanted to be different from how I was growing up. I wanted to show how I can cope with things."

"Moving across the country and settling down as a maid isn't enough?"

"Well..."

"Just take a deep breath and start afresh. There's nothing wrong with trying to be someone new, but if you work too hard at it, things are going to just be a struggle. It doesn't make you the person you really are."

Debbie still wouldn't look at him, instead focusing on his hand holding hers. She was making no effort to pull away, and Darren liked it.

"Why do you make so much sense?" Debbie murmured.

"You're the only person who's thought I speak sense."

"I'm sure that's not true."

Darren grunted. "I'm surprised you even listen to me."

"I should have listened to you from the beginning. Then maybe I wouldn't be feeling so embarrassed."

Darren didn't know what to say to that. Before he could figure out what he could say, there was a pointed cough behind him. Darren turned and saw Miranda standing in the doorway, raising her eyebrows at him. He knew a clear hint when he saw it.

"I think I'd better go." He slid off the bed, still holding onto Debbie's hand. "I'll let you rest some more."

"I'm sure I'll be up and walking around in a day or two."

"Are you sure?"

"I'm sure. This is nothing I can't handle."

Darren didn't doubt that. Debbie was known to get up and carry on moving no matter what the situation. She wasn't going to let this stop her. Then he realized he was still holding her hand. Coughing, he let go, almost dropping her hand heavily onto the bed.

"I... I'll leave you to it," he mumbled. "I... I've got... yes, I've got..."

"Darren?"

Darren was almost at the door when Debbie's voice stopped him. He turned and saw her giving him a smile.

"Thank you. I do appreciate your help."

Darren didn't know how to respond. His heart was racing just seeing her smile. Avoiding Miranda's look, he hurried from the room, almost tripping over his feet as he caught the doorframe. Biting back a groan, Darren made his way to the stairs. Oh, why did he have to forget how to walk at a moment like this?

He was sure Miranda was trying not to laugh at him as he went down the stairs.

CHAPTER NINE

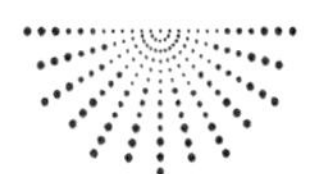

ebbie stood on the edge of the cliff and looked out across the greenery before her. The valley was looking very lush and vibrant. The sun was out and it was nice and warm. Debbie liked it when the day was like this; it made her feel better going out into the countryside and breathing in the fresh air. Having several mining shafts dotted around on the edge of the property, plus the smell from the ranch, it wasn't always easy to get any pure clean air.

But it was more than she would have gotten where she grew up. Atlanta had quite a few factories, and even though their house hadn't been that close to any of them, the smell was still there, especially the smoke.

At least they had had it better than her friends on the outskirts of their district. They lived close to a tanning yard, and the smell coming from there had been disgusting. That was not something she could get used to.

Debbie was tempted to stay out here for a while. She had the afternoon off, and she had wanted to go for a walk to clear her head. Her knee was better, although it was still a bit painful after walking so much. All she wanted to do was soak up the scenery and have time to herself.

And figure out what she was going to do regarding Darren.

Before, Debbie had been too nervous to do anything. Even with trying to be a different, more confident person, when it came to talking to men she ended up being a little nervous. Especially around Darren, which just ended up being embarrassing. Debbie had a feeling she was talking about absolute nonsense a lot of the time, and she kept stumbling over her words. Darren didn't seem to mind, though. He was very patient with her, barely batting an eyelid when Debbie sounded like a fool.

He was such a sweet man. Debbie didn't think she had come across anyone like him before. The pastor they had lived near to back in Atlanta had been about the same age, but he had been rather pious and condescending. He hadn't been particularly kind to Debbie, either. So to have Darren be the complete opposite was rather surprising. It had taken her a while to get used to it.

But she wasn't about to complain. She liked having Darren around. He made her feel happy, even if she was still embarrassing herself. Debbie liked being around him, watching him for a smile that was directed her way. To hear him talk, even if it was with his boring sermons. He was engaging, and Debbie found herself engrossed during services at the church. Much more so than she had been in the past.

Also, he was a good conversationalist outside of the church. And he actually listened. Debbie appreciated that; she had to have talked his ear off multiple times already. But Darren didn't seem to mind.

When had she started falling for him? Debbie didn't know, but something had shifted in the last eighteen months. She wasn't sure when it started; it just happened. Then it just made her feel like a little girl experiencing her first crush again. Debbie hated feeling insecure.

Then again, Darren had never made her feel insecure. Shy, yes, but not insecure.

Should she say something? All of her sisters were married now, and Debbie was feeling a little left out. She didn't want to be unmarried for the rest of her life, but could she manage as a pastor's wife? Would Darren even accept her feelings?

She wasn't even sure. Darren could have his pick of women, so why would he go for her?

Sighing, Debbie started walking again. She really needed to stop thinking about Darren so much. It was getting frustrating thinking about him all the time.

There is something you can do about it. You can tell him instead of bottling it up.

And then he'll reject me, and I'll be left alone.

You don't know, maybe it's time you find out.

Debbie sighed. Things were supposed to be more simple being out in Pine Ridge. For her, it felt like everything was getting more complicated.

She needed to head back. Her knee was beginning to hurt, and she knew it wouldn't be long before she was limping. Nothing was broken, and the bruises were fading nicely, but the whack she had experienced had made her leg feel a little delicate. The doctor had told her to not walk so much, and Debbie had walked a little further than she planned.

She was probably going to be limping for a couple of days now.

Debbie was coming to a fork in the road when she saw Andrea coming the other way. The other woman was sashaying along with a parasol to protect herself from the sun. She looked very elegant as she walked down the path.

Debbie stopped. What was Andrea doing here? As far as she was aware, Andrea didn't come out onto the property unless it was to the house. She had declared that doing anything more was pointless. And yet, she was here.

There was a path off to the left, and Debbie contemplated taking that. It took her down into the valley, and it would take longer to get back, but she was willing to do it if it meant not interacting with Andrea.

But she had barely started moving when Andrea caught up to her.

"Oh, I was wondering where you were." The other woman looked Debbie up and down. "You look worse for wear. Maybe you shouldn't go out in the sun without some proper protection."

Debbie tried not to bristle at that.

"Why are you out here, Andrea? I thought you didn't go for walks."

"I was actually looking for you." Andrea twirled the parasol on her shoulder. Debbie wished she didn't look so cool and elegant. "I wanted to tell you something, and I wasn't about to wait for you to get back."

"Why were you looking for me?"

"Because I want you to back off from Darren."

Debbie blinked. "I beg your pardon? What?"

"I want you to leave Darren alone. He's not yours, and it's clear there's something between you two." Andrea sniffed. "I don't know why he likes you, but he does. And I'm not having it."

Debbie felt her mouth drop open.

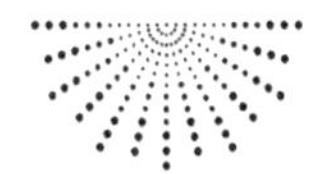

CHAPTER TEN

*D*ebbie felt like she had been hit over the head with that parasol. Then she felt indignant.

"You want me to back off from a friend? For what? Are you jealous that someone else is getting attention?"

"The only person he should be focusing on is me. I'm a much better match for him."

"Oh, are you?" Debbie folded her arms. "And what do you think you have to offer him? Because I can't see much."

Andrea snorted.

"I can offer him much more than you can. What is he going to see with someone who has no money and works as a lowly maid? That's not exactly the sort of person a man like him needs."

"And you think you can be better?"

"I know I can."

Debbie couldn't help but laugh at that. Andrea had some audacity to think she was better. It was like being back in Atlanta when the pretty girls were mean to her when she was talking to someone they liked. Evidently, that sort of petty attitude wasn't limited to the East.

"You left your father and called him names, saying he wasn't worthy to be your father. The only reason you're back is that he's got money, and you're worried that he's going to be spending it on my family to help us out."

"Everyone knows that Father's money is going to become mine. You don't deserve it."

"So, you're admitting it?"

Andrea shrugged. "It's my inheritance, besides, I'll just deny it if someone else asks. I'm just trying to reconnect with my father after being apart for years like a dutiful daughter would."

"But with me, you're willing to admit that you're worried that your inheritance is going to get smaller because your father is generous enough to help us?" Debbie snorted. "You're just a gold digger, that's all there is to it."

"What's wrong with protecting what is mine?" Andrea tucked a stray curl behind her ear and smirked. "And that includes Darren. He's mine."

"Why are you so interested in him? He clearly doesn't like you."

"Of course, he does! I've always had a bit of a thing for him. It's a shame that he's not wealthy, but he makes up for it with his looks. It's been my dream to marry him since I was thirteen and my money will make everything perfect for him. What man wouldn't want that?"

The thought of Andrea getting married to Darren made Debbie feel slightly nauseous. She slowly counted to five in her head, trying to stop her frustrations from building up and bubbling over. It worked, to some extent.

"If you've seen the way Darren is with you, you should know that getting married to him isn't going to happen. He's not going to agree to it."

"He will once Father's spoken to him."

"Alex doesn't even agree with it."

Andrea sniggered. "That's what you think. You might believe that, but Father wants the best for me. And he wants me in his life for good. By now, he knows that if I want something, I'm going to get it."

"You haven't gotten his money yet, so what makes you think you're going to get Darren?"

"At least I have a better chance than you." Andrea looked Debbie up and down. "Look at you. You're boring and your clothes are starting to look worn. They are last year's fashion, the men out here might be a little behind, but even they can tell when they compare you to me." She held her head up and even preened a little. "And you think you're better than everyone else. That's not a good look on anyone. Darren certainly doesn't like it."

"You don't know what he thinks."

"I know he's not going to choose you. You're not right to be a pastor's wife."

"And you are?"

Andrea patted her hair. "I'm perfect for it, and I know how to make a man smile. You're just an uncouth has-been who tries too hard. You'll fail before the first year is out."

Debbie had to fight down an urge to slap this woman. That would not be good luck for a pastor's wife! A giggle escaped her as she clenched her fists and took a deep breath. Some of what Andrea said was true, as such it cut deeply. But she was a better person than she had been. Losing their money had improved all of them.

However, talking to Andrea was giving her a headache, and it was making her more upset. She turned away, moving towards the path into the valley.

"I've got to get back to the house."

"Don't trip over your own feet while you're at it." Andrea giggled. "You don't want to be caught by a mountain lion, do you?"

Debbie ignored her, silently wishing that a mountain lion would appear and chase after Andrea. It was cruel, yes, but it would make her feel a little better to see Andrea in a bad situation for once. Forcing a smile on her face, she kept walking. What Andrea said meant nothing, Darren was a wise man and he would see through the other woman's wiles, or at least she hoped he would. Andrea was potentially wealthy, beautiful, and from a good family, what did she have to offer?

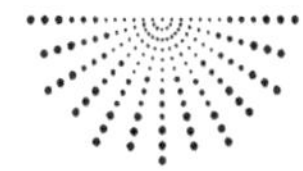

Darren had made a decision. It had taken a few days to figure out what he was going to do, but after talking to Debbie and with Alex's words going around in his head, Darren was finally sure of what he wanted.

He was going to tell Debbie how he felt. He was going to ask if she would consider marrying him. That was a bit fast, considering they hadn't actually courted or anything of the kind, but Darren was willing to take the risk. After all, he had known Debbie for well over a year. That was enough time to get to know someone, wasn't it?

His stomach churned and he felt his palms sweating as he thought about it. Was he just being a coward? Was that why he had not asked her to walk out with him?

This was silly. Dithering over everything was going to just drag it out, and Darren would let his own shyness get in the way. Alex had said a few times before that he needed to grab the proverbial bull by the horns and take charge. He was going to do it, this time around.

Now he just had to figure out how he was going to do it. Perhaps he could go up to the ranch and talk to Debbie in private, or ask her to his home for dinner. His neighbor often cooked his meals, so she would be more than happy to help; she had been pestering him to get married for years, telling him that he deserved a good woman.

Debbie would make a great pastor's wife. She wasn't the most devoted of his congregation, something Darren was well aware of. But she was kind, understanding, and listened to him and others. She was always willing to lend a hand and she was beautiful. One smile from her and the sun came out. Nothing mattered as long as she said yes.

His smile fell from his face.

There was the issue of Andrea, of course, but she couldn't complain about this, it was nothing to do with her. She had to be aware that Darren was not romantically interested in her. She was too pretentious, rude, and snobby. Darren didn't care for people like that at all. Even if he did love her, which he didn't, she would look down on his parishioners, mock their clothing and their lack of money. If she had a problem with what he wanted, that was nothing to do with him.

Yes, he was going to do this. Instead of hiding away and being nervous, Darren was going to take charge. Hopefully, Debbie would say yes.

But if she said no? Darren didn't want to think about that. His stomach felt like a big empty hole and his shoulders like they carried the world. He had to have faith that he could do this, that this was the right path.

He would go and see her this evening. After he had sorted things out for the service the next day. This one seemed to be taking a while, maybe because he kept thinking about Debbie. If he got this sermon done, Darren would be able to focus on Debbie instead of his work. Now, all he had to do was drag his mind to the sermon, he could do this in his sleep most days. He had to get a grip.

He was going to do this, he was going to tell Debbie how he felt.

Now he had made the decision, everything felt lighter and he felt a whole lot happier. Darren often talked to others about things feeling better when everything was falling into place, now, he truly understood the words he had used. This felt... right.

He couldn't wait to see Debbie, but for now, he had to work. Clearing his mind he prayed for a moment and then began to write. The sermon flowed from his pen, he could hardly dip it in the ink fast enough to keep up.

After finishing his work, Darren was putting things away and getting his jacket on when he realized that someone was in the church. He sighed. It would be typical that someone wanted his help when he had something to do.

Putting on the smile that he kept reserved for the churchgoers, Darren headed out into the church. Only to stop when he saw Andrea coming up the aisle, twirling her parasol on her shoulder. She gave him a warm, beaming smile when she saw him.

"Hey, Darren."

"Andrea? What are you doing in here?"

"Why else would I be here? I came looking for you." Andrea closed her parasol and leaned it against a pew.

"We have a few things to discuss. Things that have been on the cards for a while."

"Discuss what?"

"What else? Us."

Darren shook his head. "There's nothing to discuss. Now, if you'll excuse me? I've got things to do."

"Wait!" Andrea darted in front of him, holding up her hands so they were touching his chest. "Why can't we just sit and talk? You and I haven't done that since we were barely grown."

"That's because I didn't want to be around you." Darren knew he sounded rude, but he couldn't bring himself to be courteous. "I thought I made it clear when we were younger that I didn't care much for you."

"We were children. I'm different as an adult."

"I very much doubt it."

Andrea pouted.

"I am. I've grown a lot as a person, and I know what I want in life. I'm sure you know where this is going."

Darren did know where this was going. He sighed. "Look, Andrea, I know you think there's something between us..."

"There is, of course, there is! You and I..."

"It's all in your head. I don't know why you like me when we're very different people, but it's not going to end up with us being together."

Andrea lifted her chin. "You don't know that. Sometimes being opposite people works better in a marriage."

Darren's mouth fell open. "Did you just say marriage?"

CHAPTER TWELVE

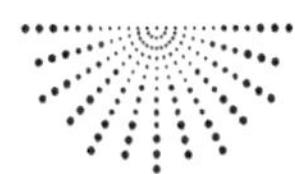

"**O**f course, marriage!" Andrea said. "That's what happens between two people, isn't it?"

Darren couldn't believe his ears. At first, he had tried to put her off politely, but more recently he had become increasingly rude. It was not something he liked to do, it did not make him feel good but he also felt it was the best way to handle this situation. How could she have ignored all he had said? "I'm not getting married to you."

Andrea flinched. "Why would you say that? You know that I love you."

"Love?" Darren couldn't stop the laugh that barked out of him. "You don't know what love is. If you did, you would have looked at your father as more than a money-pit."

"But he is a money-pit," Andrea protested. "Aren't parents supposed to provide for their children?"

"To an extent, but not when that child is... well, treats him as you do," Darren shot back. "You and your mother only wanted money. Alex is a good man, and he wanted to give you everything, but you took advantage of it. You didn't care for him at all unless he could give you something."

Andrea folded her arms. "You make it sound like I did something wrong?"

"How can you not know that you are wrong in this? No children would treat their parents like a bank. It's not all about money, it's about love as well. About respecting other people." Darren shook his head he knew he was losing his temper and he tried to haul it back in. The problem was, that he worried where this might be ending, Andrea was clearly delusional. He took a breath and spoke passionlessly. "Your mother never respected anyone, and you're just the same. You don't respect your father, nor anyone around you. And you're just down-right mean to everyone. Why would I want to marry someone who's so mean to other people?"

Andrea looked like she was beginning to falter. She looked slightly bewildered. "But... I'm not mean to other people. Why would you say that?"

"Do you think I haven't seen how you are to Debbie?"

"Debbie?" Andrea snorted, recovering some of her bravado. "She doesn't know her place. She isn't rich anymore, so she doesn't get to dictate anything. She doesn't get to swan around my house as if she owns the place.."

"I have not seen this from her. What does she dictate?" Darren demanded. "Tell me that. What does she dictate?"

Andrea hesitated. Darren sighed and stepped around her. "I'm not doing this anymore, Andrea. I know you want to be married to me, for some strange reason, but it's not going to happen. I will only marry for love."

Andrea gasped. "What?"

"I've made it clear many times that I'm not interested in anything with you, but you keep bothering me. I guess I didn't make it clear enough." Darren turned to her as Andrea tried to follow him. "I have no intention of marrying you or of having anything to do with you. Why would I be with someone whose principles and ideals are completely the opposite of mine, someone who is disrespectful towards her father, and treats everyone else as if they're beneath her? What part of that says you're perfect for me as a pastor's wife?"

Andrea's face had drained of color. Darren did feel a little bad about speaking like this, but he knew he had to put an end to this, once and for all. What's more, he wanted to go and find Debbie before the day went on for too long.

Andrea spluttered. "But... but... I love you!"

Darren was taken aback by this but, as he thought about it he knew it wasn't true. "You love yourself, nobody else. That's not for me, Andrea."

Andrea scowled. "Why are you so rude to me? You've never spoken to me like this before."

"I have been very clear with you over the years and yet, you ignore me. I need you to know that I'm not interested in entertaining you a second longer. Now, if you'll excuse me?" Darren turned away. "I've got something important to do."

"You're going to see her, aren't you?" Andrea accused. "What does she have that I don't? I can't see it."

Darren reached the door and turned back. Andrea was glaring at him. For a moment, he thought she would stamp her feet like a petulant child. All that was missing was the wobbly bottom lip.

"She has my heart. She pretty much has since she arrived. And nobody is taking that away."

Andrea stared. "You love her? That can't be! You can't love her!"

"Why not?"

"Because she's pathetic!"

Darren snorted. "You have just proven my point. If that is all you can come up with? That she's pathetic? You need to realize just how mean and childish you sound. No one is pathetic, we are all God's children and we all deserve respect."

"She's..."

"I'm not hearing it, Andrea. No more name-calling. Get out of my church, and leave me alone. And leave Debbie alone."

Andrea looked outraged. Then she recovered and smirked. "I'll leave Debbie alone. I won't need to do anything."

"What's that supposed to mean?"

"Oh, nothing. Just hope that she made it back from her walk. I know the mountain lions are out at the moment."

Darren didn't like the look in her eye. It was devious, calculating, and mean. Now he was worried about Debbie. If she was out there alone and the mountain lions were there, what could happen to her?

Turning his back on Andrea, he hurried from the church.

CHAPTER THIRTEEN

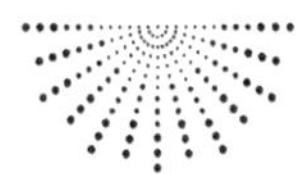

*D*ebbie's heart was pounding and her breath was coming in short sharp gasps. She worried that she might pass out. She had been trying to breathe as light as possible so the mountain lion didn't notice that she was close by, but it was getting harder with the blood racing through her veins fueled by fear. What could she do?

Now she knew that it had been a foolish idea to take the valley path. It had all to do to getting away from Andrea. Debbie had just wanted to avoid the woman, who had been very smug towards her, rushing and hurrying away had resulted in her turning over on her ankle and slipping down the slope.

As she got to the bottom of the slope she saw the remains of some meat. It looked like it had been put there, was someone luring the lions to this spot? Had Andrea done this and forced her on to this route?

No, she couldn't have. Debbie felt her panic increase. There had been sightings of mountain lions but no one really bothered. The men would simply fire a warning shot if they saw them.

Debbie took a deep breath, she had to calm down and think.

Thankfully, she hadn't fallen far, and she did land on soft grass, but moving was not that easy with a turned ankle, she was not going to be quick or agile.

Looking weak was not good when a cougar and its cubs were nearby.

Alex had warned everyone that a cougar family had come back into the valley, and to not go down there so they could keep out of the way. In her desperation to get away, Debbie had forgotten.

Now she was lying on the grass with a throbbing ankle, feeling faint, and there was a large wild animal just below her. She peered down into the valley, two little cubs were frolicking in the grass. In any other situation, that would have been very cute, but this was far too close for comfort. Debbie wanted to get out of there, but there was no chance of outrunning a mountain lion.

Lying in the grass, she silently cursed her bad luck. She should have been more responsible and just walked past Andrea instead of trying to avoid her. Instead, she had put herself in a very bad situation.

How was she going to get out of this? Was the mountain lion going to notice her? What happened then?

Debbie didn't really want to think about it. It scared her too much.

The cubs were starting to pad away, still chasing each other. Their mother was laid down, stretched out in the late afternoon sun, looking very relaxed. Debbie could only hope there wasn't a male around; she was in real trouble if it was prowling about.

Reaching for her ankle, Debbie gingerly tested it with her fingers. That throbbed a bit, but it was bearable. Then she pressed her foot into the ground. Now that hurt. She wasn't going to be moving very fast right now.

The sound of something moving just above her had Debbie freezing. Oh, no, that wasn't the male mountain lion, was it? With her heart in her mouth, Debbie looked up the slope. She almost burst into tears when she saw Darren on the path above her. He was crouched down, peering over the edge. He raised a finger to his lips and then pointed towards the lions.

Debbie looked and saw the mother had gotten to her feet, yawning with a wide mouth to show her huge teeth. Seeing those sent a shiver down her spine. Then the adult cougar started following her cubs, who were now rolling around under a tree further down the valley. They looked far enough away for her to be comfortable.

Although Debbie didn't think she would be comfortable until she was well and truly away from them.

"Debbie?" Darren whispered down to her. "Can you move?"

"I... I think so." Debbie gestured at her leg. "I hurt my ankle."

"Just take it slow."

"What if that lion comes after us?"

"Just take it slowly and quietly. We'll get away before they know what's happening."

Debbie really hoped so. She really didn't like being in this situation. Shifting carefully up onto her knees, she began to crawl up the slope. It put pressure on her bad ankle, and she had to grit her teeth to stop herself from screaming. Moving had hurt more than she expected. Taking a deep breath, she hauled herself up the slope, glancing back at the mountain lion. It was further away, and it didn't seem to be too interested in her. She had a feeling that wouldn't be the case in a moment.

"Come on, Debbie." Darren shifted onto his knees and held out a hand. "I've got you."

Debbie took his hand and tried to help as Darren pulled her up onto the path. They ended up in a heap, and then both of them froze. Darren moved carefully, leaning over Debbie to look down the slope. Debbie felt him let out a breath in relief.

"Nothing so far. We're going to have to be quiet."

"Are we going to get away?"

"We'll be fine."

Debbie didn't feel fine. She was terrified. This was not a position she wanted to find herself in.

"Debbie." Darren stroked her cheek. "Just follow me. I'll get you out of here."

"Do you promise?"

Darren didn't respond for a second. Then he pressed a quick kiss to her mouth, a fleeting movement that left Debbie momentarily stunned. Darren pulled away before she could react.

"I promise," he whispered. Then he took her hand. "Now, let's get out of here."

Debbie couldn't agree more with that. Resisting the urge to run, she allowed Darren to pull her slowly to her feet and then they headed up the slope towards the higher path. She glanced down into the valley and saw the mountain lion, now lying in a patch of sunlight while her cubs jumped on her. She didn't seem to be paying any attention to them at all. Hopefully, that would carry on until they were far away.

They climbed up the slope in silence, Darren's hand clamped around Debbie's hand so tightly she thought her fingers were going to lose any feeling in them. She could feel her heart racing so fast she was swaying as she moved. Things were getting really wonky. Debbie could only hope she didn't end up collapsing here.

Why did she have to be the clumsy one?

They reached the top of the slope. The mountain lion family looked very small far below, but Debbie wasn't about to relax. Not until they were far away. Darren seemed to be thinking the same thing, making her move along in silence until they were away from the edge. Debbie's heart was still racing quite a bit, but the dizziness had gone.

She felt like she could breathe more easily once they got the ranch house in sight. That was when Debbie's legs gave out on her, and she ended up stumbling. Darren caught her.

"Debbie?"

"I... I think I just... my ankle..."

"Does it hurt?"

Debbie nodded. Now the shock of what had happened was wearing off, and she was beginning to feel the pain in her ankle. It was too much for her, she had to bite her lip to stop herself from crying.

"Here, sit down." Darren urged her over to a patch of grass and eased her down. Then he knelt beside her. "What else did you hurt?"

"I think I knocked myself about in the fall." Debbie winced as she realized how much her body hurt. "I was just walking, and then my ankle went from under me, and I started to fall…"

"Debbie, do not worry. We're safe now." Darren brushed her hair out of her face, taking a leaf out of her locks. "You know, you're going to need a minder to make sure you don't get into trouble again."

"I can't help it if I'm clumsy."

"Why did you take that path? Alex would have told you about the mountain lions in the vicinity."

"I…" Debbie bit her lip. She was going to sound like a fool. "I came across Andrea, and I didn't want to be anywhere near her."

"Andrea?" Darren frowned. "What was she doing out there?"

"I have a feeling she was coming to look for me. We… we talked… well, I wouldn't call it talking…"

"What did she say?"

Debbie didn't know if she could tell him. It was too embarrassing in front of Darren. She looked away and blinked back her tears.

CHAPTER FOURTEEN

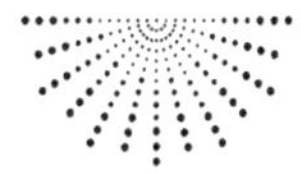

"*D*ebbie?" Darren touched her cheek, his fingers were soft against her skin. So soft, so comforting, she wanted them to stay there but he was making it hard to concentrate. "What did she say? I know she said something to you."

"I don't know if I can."

"Try."

Could she? Debbie gulped.

"She was pretty much telling me to stay away from you, and that I'm..." she sighed. "That I'm boring and pathetic. That she's going to get everything."

"She really said that?"

"Pretty much."

Darren frowned. He sat back and shook his head.

"Andrea needs to back off. I've told her as much. She doesn't get to have everything because she believes she's entitled to it."

"She seems to be under the impression that she's entitled to you."

"Well, that's not happening. I've already said that she and I are not happening, no matter what she wants."

"But..."

"I'm not a toy to be claimed and passed around to others," Darren cut her off. "I have my own opinions of people, and I want to make my own choices without being forced into it."

Debbie was confused. What was he saying?

"So... you and Andrea...?"

"What?"

"I thought... you two..."

"That we would end up together?" Darren scoffed. "Debbie, how long have you known me? You know my feelings about that woman."

"I... I thought that didn't matter."

"I don't like Andrea, and that's not happening. I'm not about to marry someone I don't like and who is very unsuitable to be my wife."

"But she's very beautiful," Debbie pointed out. "And she's so sophisticated."

"She's not a nice person, and she values money and position over everything. I don't do that." Darren leaned in. "Why would I want to be with someone when I'm in love with you?"

It took a moment for Debbie to realize what he had just said. She was sure her mind had gone blank as she stared at him.

"What did you say?"

"I think you heard me loud and clear."

Darren kissed her, cradling her head as he angled the kiss in a way that made Debbie melt into his arms. She heard someone moaning, and realized it was her. When they came up for air, his arms were around her and Debbie was clutching onto his jacket. She was also panting, suddenly feeling out of breath.

"Does that get the message across?" Darren asked, his breath tickling her mouth.

"I... I guess..." Debbie licked her lips, still feeling the press of his mouth on hers. "But... you... you never..."

"For someone so confident and outspoken, you seem to have lost the ability to speak." He chuckled.

"Well, it's not every day that someone suddenly says they love you and then kisses you." Debbie pulled back. "And this doesn't feel like you. You're not normally this forward when discussing something like love."

"Because I'm a fool. I should have done this a long time ago." Darren shifted to sit beside her. He took her hand. "I've been in love with you since we met, but you were starting somewhere new, everything was frightening, and I didn't want to make you feel overwhelmed. Then the longer you were here, the more I began to think that you were too good for me and that there wasn't going to be anything between us."

Debbie blinked. "You think I'm too good for you?"

"I believe you are."

"Even though I can injure myself just walking, and I'm hard-headed when it comes to certain things?"

"Well, that just makes you who you are. I love it, even if I do wonder about your motivations." Darren raised her hand to his mouth and kissed it. "I do love you for the person you are, Debbie. Flaws and all. The more time we spent together, the more nervous I got. I thought someone else would come along and snatch you away, as you rightly deserved. I didn't think I'd be good enough."

Debbie stared. "Seriously?"

He chuckled again and stroked his fingers across her cheek. "I believe so."

He really thought that? Debbie let that settle. All the while she thought Darren was too good for her, he was thinking the same thing about her.

"So, where does that leave us?"

"Where do you want it to leave us?" He raised an eyebrow.

That simple gesture made her stomach fill with butter-flies. "I'm not sure. I was thinking you might be able to tell me."

Darren chuckled. Then he kissed her fingers again.

"How about a wedding? I know that's where we'll end up eventually. We just took a little longer than everyone else."

"Was that a proposal?"

"I've not done it before, so I suppose it is."

Debbie couldn't help but laugh. Her shock seemed to be wearing off. She was feeling lighter, happier than before. She shuffled closer to Darren, careful with her bad ankle, and kissed him. As they pulled apart, Darren raised an eyebrow.

"Was that a yes?"

"Well, you gave me an unconventional proposal. You figure it out." Debbie tapped his mouth with her finger. "You're lucky that I love you, too, otherwise, I would be demanding that you propose to me properly."

"You really do love me?"

"Did you doubt it?"

"For a moment, I did."

"Then don't." Debbie rested her head on his shoulder. "Just be more upfront with everything in the future. I don't want to try and play a guessing game all the time."

"I won't." Darren wrapped an arm around her shoulders and kissed her head. "I promise."

Debbie didn't need to look at him to know that he meant it.

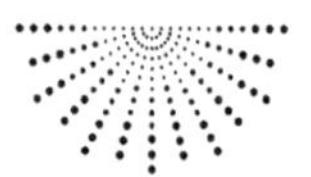

Miranda couldn't help but smile as she watched Debbie and Darren. They were talking to Darren's fellow pastor and Sheriff Nelson, Debbie looking the happiest she had seen her daughter in a long time. Darren looked equally pleased. Miranda was surprised he wasn't puffing out his chest.

At least, he had finally done something about the tension building between the two of them. Miranda had suspected something within a couple of months of coming to Pine Ridge. She knew her daughters, and she could see Debbie was gravitating towards Darren, which had been surprising given how she had always been the one looking for excitement. However, Darren was not a stuffy pastor, he was a man who could see action and stand on his own.

The more she saw of them together, the more she noted the chemistry between them, but both of them had been incredibly shy around each other. Miranda had been beginning to wonder if they were actually going to say anything, or if she would have to intervene.

Now they had, and in an awkward, but rather cute, way. It was not the most conventional way for him to propose, but Miranda wasn't about to complain. They were a good fit for each other. Debbie needed someone level-headed, and Darren would benefit from having someone who had a bit more of an adventurous spirit.

"They look like a sweet couple, don't they?"

Her heart missing a beat, Miranda turned to see Alex standing behind her. She tried not to think how handsome he looked in his best suit, freshly shaven as well. Miranda had liked the rough, scruffy look on him, which had been surprising. It wasn't something she was normally attracted to, but on Alex, it was a good look.

Why was she thinking about how attractive he was? She needed to stop doing that.

"They are," she squeaked and cleared her throat when Alex raised an eyebrow. "I think they'll be a good pairing."

"I've been telling Darren that since I figured out how he felt about Debbie, but he was too shy to do anything."

"I didn't think Darren came across as shy. Slightly awkward, maybe, but not shy." She gave him a searching look.

"Debbie turned him into an awkward man all over. Also, he's too polite with the ladies, if he wasn't, Andrea would have gotten the message a while ago."

Miranda frowned. "What's going on with Andrea now? I haven't seen her for a while."

"I think Darren told her off. She wouldn't say what happened, but she said she didn't approve of the match." Alex shrugged. "She did tell me that I had to do something about it, but I just pointed out that neither of them are my children, so I'm not doing anything."

"How did she react to that?"

"She said that she hated me and ran away. It was pretty much the same as normal when she doesn't get her own way."

"And you're not upset about it?"

"She's made her position clear with regards to me. While I do love her as my daughter, I don't like her as a person."

Miranda could understand, although she didn't really approve. She couldn't imagine disliking one of her own children.

"I must say that I'm impressed with your family, Miranda," Alex went on.

"What do you mean?"

"You came here to look for husbands and start a new life. You've managed that with all of your children now."

Miranda folded her arms.

"You make it sound like I used them as a sort of trade."

"What? No!"

"After the initial disaster, I didn't plan to look for husbands for my daughters. That was just a good thing... if it happened."

Alex arched an eyebrow. "Did I make it sound like a bad thing?"

"Yes."

"Why do you turn around everything I say, Miranda? I feel like you keep looking for an excuse to have an argument with me."

"You think that?" She took in a breath, had she been awkward?

"You've been like that since I rescued you from Jago's little auction." Alex folded his arms. "Why do you keep behaving like this? I got you out of a bad situation, and you seem to think I'm going to attack you at any moment."

Miranda faltered. This was the first time Alex had actually confronted her on her attitude. He seemed to have let it wash over him before, but not now. And now Miranda didn't know what to say.

How do you say to someone that you're in love with them but you hate that you are?

"What's wrong with us, Miranda?" Alex stepped towards her. "What happened that made you hate me?"

"I... what?" Miranda gulped. He was too close for comfort, but she couldn't bring herself to move away. "What makes you think I hate you?"

"I see it in the way you look at me, snap at me, avoid me! What did I do to you?"

"I..."

Miranda glanced around. They were just off from the rest of the wedding party. Nobody seemed to be paying any attention to either of them. She smoothed her damp palms on her skirts.

"I don't hate you."

"Do you not?"

"No."

Alex stared at her for a moment. Then he was kissing her. Miranda was so surprised that she didn't get a chance to react. Alex pretty much claimed her, holding her head still as he kissed her. He was showing who was in charge.

And Miranda didn't want him to stop.

Then he was breaking away before she could gather her thoughts. His eyes were blazing fire as he looked at her, the heat making Miranda shiver.

"I believe you," he murmured. "You don't hate me."

"Alex?"

Then Alex was letting go of her, stepping around her before striding over to Darren. Miranda watched him go, feeling her legs wobble and her mouth throb at the memory of the kiss. What had just happened there? That was probably the most confusing conversation she had ever had with Alex. Neither of them had really made sense, and then he had kissed her.

After losing her husband, she had told herself that she wouldn't get close to anyone again, and certainly not Alex Westerman. That had gone out of the window.

Now she didn't know what to do.

If you enjoyed this book you can read book 5 A Bride for the Rancher here

Miriam Wiggins inhaled deeply, as she watched the passing trees from the small window of the stagecoach. Looking down at Lucy's head on her chest, she wondered how the other woman didn't hear the rapid sound of her palpitating heart. Miriam ran one hand through her blonde hair, further disheveling it, while she patted Lucy's shoulder with the other. Lucy was already scared as it was, and if Miriam showed any signs of fear, it was going to affect Lucy too. Miriam didn't want that. She had to be strong for both of them. Even if it meant putting on a brave face.

"Miriam?" Lucy called softly.

"Yes, Lucy. What is it?" Miriam asked.

Lucy lifted her head and locked her brown eyes with Miriam's blue ones. Her brown hair was long and straight and had been put up in a bun that was managing the journey much better than Lucy's fine and flyaway hair. "Do you think they will like us?"

Miriam sighed. This was the fear that had kept them both awake throughout the long journey west. Would the men they had been sold to as mail order brides like them? Would they have gentle hearts or would they be as cold as ice? "I think I would prefer they respected us, Lucy. But we can't predict how they will react." *Why had she said that?* Keeping expectations low was a good way to prevent further disappointment, but it would not boost her friend's confidence.

"That is the least I want," Lucy said. "If we are to live as husband and wife, they could at least like us. That way, we'll be comfortable at the very least. How are we going to live with people who don't like us? It'll be miserable."

"We'll know when we get there," Miriam said. "Don't worry about that now. We need to wait and see."

Lucy gently shook her head. "I can't believe Mrs. Lauretta actually sold us as brides."

Lucy's statement made Miriam chuckle. "Really, Lucy? You can't believe it?"

Lucy smiled. "Oh, well, yes, of course, I can." Her slim eyebrows raised on a pale face. "But still, it happened sooner than I thought it would. We weren't any trouble. Why were we the first on her list? I understand that they didn't like us, but they didn't have to make it so obvious. Did you see the look on Ruth's face when our departure was announced? She was smirking."

Miriam smiled. The orphanage had been hard and though she was glad to be out of there it would have been nice to make the move themselves. To have had some control over what happened. Her stomach rolled and her heart beat against her chest like a racing horse, but she must not show her own fear. Lucy had a very good reason to fear what her intended would think. Miriam would do her best to help her friend but she may not be able to. "I knew it was going to happen months ago. Besides, we couldn't live at the orphanage forever. We both turn seventeen in a couple of months. It was time to start thinking of our own path in life."

Lucy harumphed.

"I know, Mrs. Lauretta took care of that for us, so... here we are. We're going to be fine, trust me. Aren't you at least glad we aren't at the orphanage anymore?"

"I should be," Lucy said with a smile. "But I think I'm mostly glad that I'm with you. Thankfully, we'll live in Fairplay together. I don't know what I would have done if Mrs. Lauretta sent us to different towns."

Miriam stroked Lucy's hair and sighed. It was true that no one really liked them back at the orphanage. And it was probably because of this shared adversity that she and Lucy became inseparable, like sisters. The women didn't like Miriam because she wasn't fond of cooking, sewing, or other domestic chores of that sort. They also saw Miriam as unnecessarily difficult, when, in fact, all she did was speak up for herself and Lucy. But Miriam didn't mind that. In fact, she had long chosen to be optimistic and now held the faith that leaving the orphanage was a good thing. She couldn't deny her fear of the unknown, but she would make this work, she would make it better. Once more a sliver of fear stabbed her in the gut. What if life in Fairplay was worse than life at the orphanage?

"Miriam, do you think my intended is going to accept me?" Lucy asked, stroking her elbow. "What if he doesn't want me because…"

Lucy fell silent and her gaze dropped to the nub where her left hand used to be. Lucy was missing a hand.

"Lucy, come on."

"Oh, you know it's something I should be worried about," Lucy said. "I've been bullied half my life for it and I still get bullied. My intended might think I'm no use because I don't have two hands. I should be worried about it, shouldn't I?"

"No!" Miriam groaned. "It doesn't matter. It shouldn't matter. Besides, Mrs. Lauretta would have informed your intended already before sending us to the town. Don't worry about trivial things, just keep an open mind."

Lucy sighed. "She would have told him, wouldn't she?"

"Yes. Now rest. You didn't sleep at all last night because of your worrying and you are at it again. We will soon arrive in Fairplay. I'll wake you once we get there." Miriam gave her a bright smile that she hoped looked genuine.

"Thank you, Miriam," Lucy said, nodding. "We're going to be fine. I'm going to try and be optimistic."

"That's the spirit."

Lucy dropped her head back to Miriam's shoulder and closed her eyes. Miriam stroked Lucy's dark brown hair and stared out of the window. Lucy was subtly quivering, and she let out deep sighs at intervals. Miriam could easily sense her fear and she understood it. She wasn't in a good position to dish out advice or words of encouragement, especially when she had her heart in her mouth. She had learned at a young age not to show fear else she would be deemed weak. But Miriam was scared to bits. She didn't know what to expect in Fairplay. It was the first time that she had left the orphanage and she feared that life was about to get worse.

Lucy slowly began to relax in Miriam's arms, she was starting to fall asleep. They both needed the rest but Miriam decided it was best if she stayed awake. They had been traveling for so long, and soon they were going to meet their intended grooms. Miriam could only imagine what the men looked like, what they would be like. All she knew was a name.

"It'll be fine," Miriam whispered. "It has to be."

* * *

Grab all 30 books in this great value box set for FREE with Kindle Unlimited. Love, Heart, and Family 30 Book Inspirational Collection

The Brides of Broken Bow

If you missed any of this series, all three books are now available.
Each book covers one couple and is a complete story.

God bless,

Indiana Wake

Indiana Wake was born in Denver, Colorado, where she learned to love the outdoors and horses. At the age of eleven, her parents moved to the United Kingdom to follow her father's career.

It was a strange and foreign new world, and it took a while for her to settle down. Her mom raised horses and Indiana soon learned to ride. She would often escape on horseback imagining she was back in the Wild West. As well as horses, Indiana escaped into fiction and dreamed of all the friends she had left behind.

From an early age, she loved stories. They were always sweet and clean and, more often than not, included horses, cowboys and most importantly of all a happy ever after. As she got older, she would often be found making up her own stories and would tell them to anyone who would listen.

As she grew up, she continued to write, but marriage and a job stole some of her dreams. Then one day she was discussing with a friend at church, how hard it was to get sweet and clean fiction. Though very shy about her writing Indiana agreed to share one of her stories. That friend loved the story and suggested she publish it on kindle. Together they worked really hard, and the rest, as they say, is history.

Indiana has had multiple number one bestsellers and now makes her living from her writing. She believes she was truly blessed to be given this opportunity and thanks each and every one of her readers for making her dream come true.

www.ingramcontent.com/pod-product-compliance
Lightning Source LLC
Chambersburg PA
CBHW052105150726

48002CB00006B/2234